Katie AND THE DINOSAURS

JAMES MAYHEW

ORCHARD

For Robert, Rebecca, Victoria
and my goddaughter Elizabeth

J.M.

If you would like to know how to say the
names of all the dinosaurs in the story,
please turn to the back of the book.

ORCHARD BOOKS
First published in 1991 by Orchard Books.
First published in paperback in 1994.

15

This edition published in 2014.
Text and Illustrations © James Mayhew, 1991/2014

The rights of James Mayhew to be identified as the author and illustrator of this work have
been asserted by him in accordance with the Copyright, Designs and Patents act, 1988.
A CIP catalogue record for this book is available from the British Library.

ISBN 9781408331910

Printed in China

Orchard Books
An imprint of Hachette Children's Group
Part of Hodder & Stoughton Limited
Carmelite House
50 Victoria Embankment
London EC4Y 0DZ

An Hachette UK Company
www.hachette.co.uk

www.hachettechildrens.co.uk

"COME AND LOOK, GRANDMA. Come and see
the dinosaurs!" said Katie.
Katie loved the Natural History Museum,
and she wanted to show her grandma everything.
"They're just a load of old bones," said Grandma.
"Well, you're really old," said Katie. "There must
have been dinosaurs alive when you were little."

"I'm not that old!" snorted Grandma, looking for
somewhere to sit down. They found a seat next to a
skeleton of a very fierce-looking dinosaur.
"Why don't you go and look at your horrible dinosaurs
while I have forty winks," said Grandma.
"They're not horrible," sniffed Katie. "But I do wish
they weren't just skeletons." And she skipped off on her own,
taking her picnic lunch with her, just in case she got hungry.

Katie saw all sorts of dinosaurs. Some had spikes,
others had horns or wings or long, long tails.
She closed her eyes and tried to imagine they were
alive. She thought they must have been very frightening
with their sharp teeth and claws.

Next to one of the dinosaurs was a corridor.

Katie set off down it to make sure she hadn't missed anything worth seeing.

The corridor was long and dark, and there was no one in sight. Katie began to feel scared. She looked for a *Way Out* sign, but there didn't seem to be one. She was lost.

"Now what do I do?" said Katie crossly.

She came to a big door with a notice on it that said:

ABSOLUTELY NO ADMITTANCE WHATSOEVER

"I'll just take a quick look," said Katie and she opened the door and stepped through.

The door led outside and there in front of her was a dinosaur!
It was no bigger than Katie, but it was a real live one!

"Hello," said Katie. "Who are you?"

"Hadrosaurus," said the dinosaur. "Who are you?"

"I'm Katie," said Katie, "and I think I'm lost."

"I'm lost too," said Hadrosaurus. "I was chased by
a Tyrannosaurus Rex."

"Isn't that the really fierce dinosaur?" asked Katie.

"That's right," said Hadrosaurus. "Now I don't know how to get home."

"Don't worry," said Katie. "I'll be able to see where we are from the top of this hill," and she clambered up a steep slope.

"This isn't a hill!" said Hadrosaurus, scrambling up behind her.

Katie gasped. "Oh, it's an Apatosaurus!"
She was very high up and she could see for miles.

"Now show me where you live," said Katie.
"I think it's somewhere over there, along the river bank," said Hadrosaurus.
Katie looked across the river. "What are those funny-looking birds?" she asked.
"Pterosaurs!" said Hadrosaurus. "Watch out!"

One of the Pterosaurs spotted Katie's yellow scarf.
It swooped towards her and, before Katie could duck,
it had snatched the scarf from her.
"Hey, that's mine! Bring it back!" yelled Katie.

But the Pterosaur flew far away. The Apatosaurus started moving. She was getting fed up with those two noisy creatures jumping about on her back.

The Apatosaurus lumbered down to the river for a nice cool bathe. She was so huge that Katie and Hadrosaurus just hung on and hardly got wet at all.

Katie looked across the water. All sorts of strange creatures were swimming there. She recognised some of them from the museum – the Ichthyosaurs with their long snouts, and a Plesiosaurus with its snakelike neck.

Before long, the Apatosaurus reached the edge of the water.
"Let's go," said Katie. Followed by Hadrosaurus, she slid all
the way down to the tip of the Apatosaurus's tail and they
landed in a giggling heap on the ground.
"Which way now?" said Katie.
"Into the jungle," said Hadrosaurus.

The jungle was hot and sticky. Through the trees, Katie could see a herd of enormous dinosaurs.

"What on earth are those?" asked Katie.

"I don't like the look of *them*."

"Only Stegosaurs," said Hadrosaurus.

"They won't hurt us."

"Are you sure?" said Katie, as one Stegosaur licked its lips.

"Oh, yes. They only eat plants," said Hadrosaurus. So Katie gave them some grass and then they went on through the jungle.

Suddenly Hadrosaurus let out a squeal!
There was his family! They hugged him and
they hugged Katie too for bringing him home.

"I hope you're not going to eat me," worried Katie.

"Of course not," said Hadrosaurus. "We're plant eaters too."

That reminded Katie that she hadn't eaten her lunch yet.

She was feeling quite hungry by now, but she politely shared her cucumber sandwiches and chocolate biscuits. She saved her meat pie for later.
Plant-eating dinosaurs from far and wide picked up the smell of Katie's sandwiches, and padded across the rocks towards her.

There was a spiky Styracosaurus, and a Triceratops
with his horns, the Iguanodon with his sharp thumbs
and all kinds of Ankylosaurs.
The dinosaurs shook some strange-looking fruits
out of the trees, and they all ate until they were full.
It was the best picnic Katie had ever had.

Suddenly, another dinosaur crashed out of the jungle. It was Tyrannosaurus Rex! He had been following Katie and Hadrosaurus. He grunted and growled and ground his teeth, and swished his tail and stamped his scaly feet. He was hungry! And he didn't want cucumber sandwiches or chocolate biscuits, he wanted meat! He wanted Katie! "Quick, run for your life!" said Hadrosaurus.

Tyrannosaurus Rex thundered after Katie and the
dinosaurs as they ran through the jungle towards
the river.
Katie was out of breath, but she kept on running.

At last she could see the museum ahead of her.
If only she had stayed safely inside!
Then she remembered the meat pie. She tore open her
lunch box and threw a piece at the Tyrannosaurus Rex.

The Tyrannosaurus stopped in his tracks. He sniffed
the piece of pie. He ate it up. He liked it so much that
Katie threw him the rest, even though she had been
saving it for herself. And the Tyrannosaurus Rex padded
off into the jungle again, clutching Katie's lunch box.
"Whew! That was close!" said Katie.

It was getting late now, so Katie turned to say goodbye
to Hadrosaurus.

"I do wish you could come home with me," she said,
"but Grandma would only scream and make a fuss."

"I'm happy here with my family anyway," said Hadrosaurus.
He gave Katie a lick. "Thank you for helping me find them."

"BLEAGH!" spluttered Katie, as dinosaurs have
very sloppy tongues.

Then she went back through the museum door. This time
Katie easily found her way back to Grandma, who was
waiting where she had left her.

"Where on earth have you been?" asked Grandma.

"I've seen all kinds of dinosaurs," said Katie.

"Why don't you come and have a look too?"

"All right," said Grandma. "Where do we start?"

"This way," said Katie, and, taking her hand,
off they went.

Hadrosaurus
(HAD-row-SORE-us)

Get creative with Katie!

Ankylosaurus
(An-KIE-loh-sore-us)

Here are all the dinosaurs I met in this book, and underneath each one is a guide on how to say their names.

Plesiosaurus
(PLEE-see-oh-sore-us)

Dinosaurs came in all shapes and sizes – some had spikes, others had fins, some had very long necks, and some had terribly sharp teeth. I've had a go at inventing my own dinosaur. I called it the 'Katiesaurus'! Do you like it? Why don't you draw a picture of your own imaginary dinosaur? Don't forget to give it a name!

Tyrannosaurus Rex
(Tie-RAN-oh-sore-us Rex)

Iguanodon
(Ig-WHA-noh-don)

Love Katie x

Stegosaurus
(STEG-oh-SORE-us)

Ichthyosaurus
(IK-thee-oh-sore-us)

Apatosaurus
(ah-PAT-oh-sore-rus)

Pterosaur
(TER-oh-sore)

Styracosaurus
(Sty-RAK-oh-sore-us)

Katiesaurus
(KAY-tee-sore-us)

Triceratops
(Tri-SERRA-tops)